a minedition book

published by Penguin Young Readers Group

Illustrations copyright © 2006 by Sarah Emmanuelle Burg
Original title: "Secret d'Amour" by François Garagnon, Éditions Monte-Cristo (France).
Redesigned by Michael Neugebauer
Coproduction with Michael Neugebauer Publishing Ltd., Hong Kong.
Rights arranged with "minedition" Rights and Licensing AG, Zurich, Switzerland.

Published simultaneously in Canada.
Manufactured in Hong Kong by Wide World Ltd.
Typesetting in Veljovic and Ex Ponto by Jovica Veljovic.

Library of Congress Cataloging-in-Publication Data available upon request.

ISBN 0-698-40050-X
10 9 8 7 6 5 4 3 2 1
First Impression

For more information please visit our website: www.minedition.com

The Secret of Love

Sarah Emmanuelle Burg

minedition

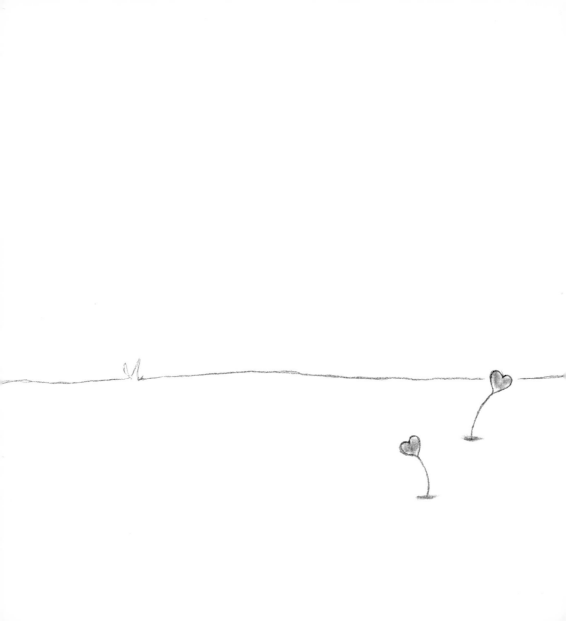

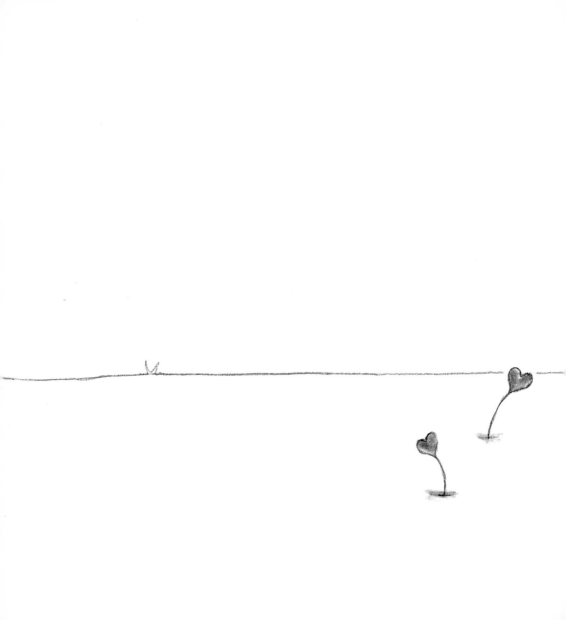